COOKIES

Bite-Size Life Lessons

written by
Amy Krouse
Rosenthal

illustrated by
Jane Dyer

HarperCollinsPublishers

Library of Congress Cataloging-in-Publication Data

Rosenthal, Amy Krouse.   Cookies : bite-size life lessons / written by Amy Krouse Rosenthal ;
    illustrated by Jane Dyer.—1st ed.   p.   cm.

ISBN-10: 0-06-058081-X (trade bdg.) — ISBN-10: 0-06-058082-8 (lib. bdg.)

ISBN-13: 978-0-06-058081-0 (trade bdg.) — ISBN-13: 978-0-06-058082-7 (lib. bdg.)

1. Conduct of life—Miscellanea.   2. Cookies—Miscellanea.   I. Title.   BJ1595.R57 2006

179'.9--dc22   2005015134   CIP AC

Typography by Carla Weise

2 3 4 5 6 7 8 9 10

❖

First Edition

For my dad, who lectured—I mean taught me—
the meanings of so many of these words . . .
and who just plain loves cookies
(oatmeal and devil's food)
—A.K.R.

For my dear friend John Kellogg
—J.D.

COOPERATE means,

How about you add the chips while I stir?

PATIENT means

waiting and waiting for the cookies to be done.

A few more minutes.

Aren't I waiting so nicely?

Still waiting.

PROUD means,
My chin is high, and I sure do like
the way my cookies turned out.

MODEST means

you don't run around telling everyone you make

the best cookies, even if you know it to be true.

RESPECT means
offering the very first cookie
to your grandmother.

TRUSTWORTHY means,

If you ask me to hold your cookie
until you come back, when you come back,
I will still be holding your cookie.

FAIR means,

You get a bite, I get a bite,

you get a big bite, I get a big bite.

UNFAIR means,

You get a bite, and now I get the rest.

COMPASSIONATE means,

Don't worry, it's okay.
You can have part of my cookie.

GREEDY means

taking all the cookies for myself.

Hee Hee Hee *Yum Yum Yum*

GENEROUS means
offering some to others.

Please take one.

You too.

Anyone else
want a cookie?

PESSIMISTIC means,

How awful, how absolutely dreadful—
I have only half my cookie left.

OPTIMISTIC means,

*This is great—
I still have half my cookie left.*

POLITE means,

Excuse me,

can you please pass the cookies?

Thank you.

HONEST means,

I have to tell you something.

The butterfly didn't really take the cookie—I took the cookie.

COURAGEOUS means,

It was not easy for me to tell you that I took the cookie, but I took a deep breath . . . and made the words come out.

ENVY means,

I can't stop looking at your cookie
out of the corner of my eye—
it looks so much better than my cookie.

Boy, I wish it were mine and not yours.

LOYAL means

that even though the new person has a much bigger cookie,

I'm sticking by you and your little cookies
because you're my very best friend.

OPEN-MINDED means,

I've never seen cookies like that before, but, uh, sure, I'll try one.

REGRET means,

I really wish I didn't eat so many cookies.

CONTENT means

sitting on the steps—just you, me, and a couple of cookies.

WISE means,

I used to think I knew everything about cookies,
but now I realize I know about one teeny chip's worth.